S0-BSD-779

SNAKEY
RIDDLES

SNAKEY RIDDLES

by Katy Hall and Lisa Eisenberg

pictures by Simms Taback

Dial Books for Young Readers / New York

Dial easy-to-read

E 818

JUL 1 3 '90

Published by Dial Books for Young Readers
A Division of Penguin Books USA Inc.
2 Park Avenue
New York, New York 10016

Published simultaneously in Canada
by Fitzhenry & Whiteside Limited, Toronto

Text copyright © 1990 by Katy Hall and Lisa Eisenberg
Pictures copyright © 1990 by Simms Taback
All rights reserved
Printed in Hong Kong by
South China Printing Company (1988) Limited

The Dial Easy-to-Read logo is a registered trademark of
Dial Books for Young Readers,
a division of Penguin Books USA Inc.,
® TM 1,162,718.

Library of Congress Cataloging in Publication Data
Hall, Katy. Snakey riddles /
by Katy Hall and Lisa Eisenberg; illustrated by Simms Taback.
p.   cm.
Summary: An illustrated collection of riddles about
snakes, including "What kind of snake do you find on
the front of your car? A windshield viper!"
ISBN 0-8037-0669-3
ISBN 0-8037-0670-7 (lib. bdg.)
1. Riddles, Juvenile. 2. Snakes—Juvenile humor.
[1. Snakes—Wit and humor. 2. Riddles.] I. Eisenberg, Lisa.
II. Taback, Simms, ill. III. Title.
PN6371.5.H35 1990 818'.5402—dc19 88-23687 CIP   AC

First Edition
E
1 3 5 7 9 10 8 6 4 2

The art for each picture was prepared using black ink,
watercolor, and colored pencils. It was then
camera-separated and reproduced in red, blue,
yellow, and black halftones.

Reading Level 2.8

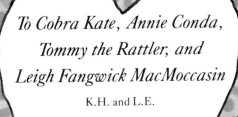

To Cobra Kate, Annie Conda,
Tommy the Rattler, and
Leigh Fangwick MacMoccasin

K.H. and L.E.

For Rachel,
the Charmer

S.T.

What kind of shoes
do reptiles wear?

Snakers!

What do little rattlesnakes like best in school?

Hisssss-tory!

What kind of snake
do you find on
the front of your car?

A windshield viper!

Why doesn't the cobra
call his mother collect?

He likes to call
poison-to-poison!

How can you revive a snake
that looks dead?

With mouse-to-mouth
resuscitation!

What kind of snake
says "Meow!"?

A snake in disguise!

How did the snakes
bust out of jail?

They scaled the wall!

13

What kind of slippers
do snakes wear?

Water moccasins!

Why did the snake
love to do arithmetic?

He was a good little adder!

Why did the
second-grade snakes
get into trouble in school?

They were always hiss-pering!

What do snakes put
on their kitchen floors?

Rep-tiles!

What does a polite snake
say after he bites you?

Fangs a lot!

What do thirsty hawks order at the soda fountain?

Chocolate milk snakes!

Why didn't the coyote
believe the snake?

It spoke with a forked tongue.

What did the hungry snake say to the snapping turtle?

"Let's go out for a bite!"

What snake has scales,
a long tongue, and flies?

A dead snake!

How do you measure a snake?

In inches.
They don't have any feet!

23

In what river are you
sure to find snakes?

The Hississippi!

Why didn't the owl
eat the green snake?

He was waiting for it to ripen!

What did the snake say
when it stopped biting
the giraffe's neck?

"It's been nice gnawing you!"

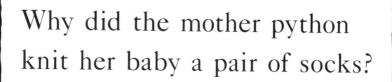

Why did the mother python knit her baby a pair of socks?

The doctor said he had grown two feet!

What did the lizard
call the snake that said,
"I'm gonna tell!"

A rattler tattler!

Why was the little snake
happy he wasn't poisonous?

Because he just bit his tongue!

How did the boa constrictor
sign his letter to the goat?

"With lots of hugs..."

What will you get
if you put a snake
in your bathtub?

Ring around the tub!

What do you get
if you cross a rattler
with a string of pearls?

A pain in the neck!

If you crossed a snake
and a robin,
what bird would you get?

A swallow!

Why did the neighbors
get tired of
the anaconda's music?

Because all he could
play were his scales!

If a forty-foot python
marries a fifty-foot
boa constrictor,
what do you get?

A long wedding!

What do you have to know
to teach a snake tricks?

More than the snake!

Why is the letter A
like a mouse?

Because it can be found
in the middle of S-N-A-K-E!

What would you get
if you crossed a watchdog
with a rattlesnake?

A very worried mailman!

Did you hear about
the two snakes that met
in the revolving door?

They started going
around together!

What does a chicken say
when it's introduced
to a boa constrictor?

Squeezed to meet you!

What does a boa constrictor
say when it's introduced
to a chicken?

Pleased to eat you!

What did the policeman
say to the angry snake?

Don't get hiss-terical!

What did the cobra say
to the flute player?

Charmed to meet you!

What is long,
thin, slithery, and
doesn't eat mice?

A snake on a diet!

What newspaper
do reptiles read?

The Scaly Daily!

What do you get
if you cross a snake
and a weenie?

The world's longest hot dog!

What would you get if
you crossed a newborn snake
with a basketball?

A bouncing baby boa!

Why shouldn't you grab
a snake's tail?

It's only his tail
but it could be *your* end!

W 2/2017   ENF 7ERNF

7-90